CLOSURE, LIMITED

CLOSURE, LIMITED

And Other Zombie Tales

Max Brooks

Duckworth Overlook

First published in 2012 by
Duckworth Overlook
90-93 Cowcross Street
London EC1M 6BF
Tel: 020 7490 7300
Fax: 020 7490 0080
info@duckworth-publishers.co.uk
www.ducknet.co.uk

A catalogue record for this book is available
from the British Library

ISBN 978-0-7156-4293-1

Typeset by Ray Davies
Printed and bound in the UK by
CPI Group (UK) Ltd, Croydon, Surrey

Contents

To Michelle Kholos Brooks,
who makes everything possible.

Introduction

The zombies came for me. I certainly wasn't looking for them. It was sometime in 1985. I was somewhere between 12 and 13 years old. My parents had just got something called 'cable TV' and according to the schoolyard rumour mill, this new invention sometimes showed real women willing to take their shirts off for no particular reason! Every time my parents went out to dinner, I made a beeline for their bedroom. I sat in front of that screen with the patience of a Buddhist monk. I waited, I hoped, I prayed, and then one night, it happened. There she was, a real live woman, completely naked! She was walking through some tropical village as the natives danced around her. As my adolescent brain tried to comprehend what my eyes were harvesting, all I could think of was 'My life has changed forever'. I had no idea how right I was.

They came out of the darkness, shambling, moaning suddenly… the party was over.

My memories are hazy from that moment on. Mostly they consist of nightmare flashes of screaming people being grabbed, their flesh torn and eaten. I remember a small animal (a cat?) leaping from the corpse of an old woman. I remember an ashen cadaver with dried blood hanging from the lips. I remember a national leader pleading for help while the other UN Delegates argue fecklessly about solutions. Most of all, I remember THEM. Mindless, slow, completely inhuman. They reminded me of a movie I'd seen recently about a giant shark that one character had called 'an eating machine'. They reminded me of a movie about a killer cyborg that 'doesn't feel pity or remorse or fear and absolutely will not stop, ever!' They reminded me of a very real plague that was now ripping through my parents' world and killing their friends in droves. They were the worst terror I could have imagined. They were zombies.

The movie I'd seen that night was called *Night of the Zombies*, and I'm 99.9% sure that the filmmakers mixed actual documentary cannibal footage into their tour de force. Whether that's true or not, each frame was burned into my adolescent brain. For years I remained haunted by these inhuman and, I thought, invincible abominations. The humans in the movie seemed powerless before their carnivorous onslaught. Wouldn't the same be true of me? That was the fate I had resigned myself to until him!

His name is George A. Romero and his movie is called *Night of the Living Dead*. I must have been 17 or 18 when I saw it, now in my own room with my own cable TV and, I'm sure, no less obsessed with shirtless women than I was at the dawn of puberty. I thought I'd put my zombie nightmares behind me, and now here they were again! The flesh eaters were back, and no less ravenous than their Italian cousins. Just like before, I was terrified by the carnage unfolding before me, and just like last time, I could not look away.

But then it dawned on me, this movie had something completely absent from that exploitative nihilistic Euro blood orgy. This movie had HOPE! Suddenly there were rules, concrete boundaries that delineated the strengths and weaknesses of the attackers. They weren't as smart as us, or as strong, or as fast. Most importantly, they could be stopped! One bullet to the brain, that's all it took! And suddenly I got it! The terror wasn't the zombies, it was our own inability to deal with them! That wouldn't be me! I'd make the right decisions. I'd do my homework. I wouldn't surrender to stupidity or fear. When they came for me, I would do whatever it took to survive!

A lifetime later, as the world braced for the all but inevitable Y2K apocalypse, I found myself reading an ever-growing stack of disaster preparedness manuals and thinking 'What about zombies?' Surely someone must have written a book on how to survive an attack by the living dead. Surely some obsessive compulsive nerd with far too much time on his hands must have asked himself 'what if' enough times to do something about it. As luck would have it, that obsessive compulsive nerd turned out to be me.

I never expected *The Zombie Survival Guide* to be published. I wrote it to read it. The living dead continue to fascinate (and terrify) me, and the older I get the greater my obsession grows. Zombies are a global phenomenon, the perfect lens for examining societal collapse. They are SARS, they are AIDS. They are the hurricane that drowned an entire city, or the 'master race' that burned an entire continent. They are an existential threat, a slate wiper, and have an ability to expose our own suicidal weaknesses; I'll never lose my fear of them.

Closure, Limited:
A Story of World War Z

BERUFJORDUR, ICELAND

*Thomas Kiersted looks exactly like his prewar picture. His
frame may have thinned considerably, and his salt-and-
pepper hair may have lost all its pepper, but his eyes show
no trace of 'survivors' stare.' He waves to me from the deck
of* The African Queen. *The three-hundred-foot former
sailing yacht is still a magnificent vessel, despite her patched
sails and naval grey paintwork. This former plaything of the
Saudi royal family now flies the flag of the European Union
and is the mobile headquarters of 'Closure Limited.'*

Welcome aboard! *Doctor Kiersted holds out a hand
as the supply launch pulls alongside.* Quite a party, eh? *He
refers to the collection of warships and troop transports
anchored in the fjord.* Good thing for us this is only a
recce expedition. It's getting harder and harder to
secure our subjects. South and East Asia are secure,
Africa's drying up. Russia used to be our best exporter,
unofficially, of course, but now… They really mean it,
closing their borders. No more 'flexible negotiations,'

not even on the individual level. What's this world coming to when you can't bribe a Russian?

He chuckles as we head below to B deck. A loud commotion roars down the passageway from a lit hatchway.

No, it's not that. *Kiersted gestures over his shoulder.* Cricket season, Sri Lanka versus the West Indies. We get the BBC live feed directly from Trinidad. No, our subjects are all kept below in specially modified cabins. Not cheap, but nothing we do here is.

We descend to C deck, past crew cabins and various equipment lockers. Officially our funding comes from the EU Ministry of Health. They provide the ship, the crew, a military liaison to help collect subjects, or, if no troops are available, enough money to pay for private contractors like 'the Impisi', you know, the 'Hyenas.' They don't come cheap either.

None of our public funding comes from America. I watched the debates your Congress had on C-SPAN. I cringed when that one senator tried to support it openly. He is now, what, working as an underling in your Department of National Graves Registration?

The irony is most of our money comes from America, from private individuals or charities. Your *name removed for legal reasons* set up the fund that's given dozens of your countrymen a chance to use our services. We need every dollar, or Cuban peso, I should say, the only money that really means anything now.

It's difficult and dangerous to collect subjects, very dangerous, but that part of the process is relatively inexpensive. The preparation—that is where the real money goes. It's not enough to just find a subject with the right height, build, gender, and reasonably close facial features. Once we have them—*he shakes his head*—then the real work begins.

Hair has to be cleaned, cut, possibly dyed. Most of the time facial features have to be reconstructed or else actually sculpted from scratch. We have some of the best specialists in Europe and America. Most of them work for standard wages, or even 'pro bono,' but some know exactly how much their talent is worth and charge for every second of their time. Talented bastards.

We come to E deck, now closed off by an armoured

hatch guarded by two large armed men. Kiersted speaks to them in Danish. They nod, then look at me. My apologies, he says, I don't make the rules. I show my ID, both U.S. and UN, a signed copy of my legal disclaimer, and my letter of consent, stamped with the seal of the European Union's Minister of Mental Health. The guards examine them closely, even using prewar ultraviolet lights, then nod to me and open the door. *Kiersted and I pass into an artificially lit passageway. The air is still, odourless, and extremely dry. I hear the thrum of either several small or one extremely large and powerful dehumidifier. The hatches on either side of us are solid steel, opened only by electronic key, and warning in several languages for unauthorized personnel to stay out. Kiersted lowers his voice slightly.* This is where it happens. Preparation. I am sorry we can't enter; a safety issue for the workers, you understand.

We continue down the passageway. Kiersted gestures to the doors without touching them. Face and hair are only part of the preparation. 'Wardrobe personalization'— that is a challenge. The process simply won't work if the subjects are, say, wearing the wrong clothes or missing some kind of personal item. Here, at least, we can thank globalization. The same T-shirt, say, made in China, could be found in Europe, America, anywhere. The same for electronic items, or jewellery; we have a jeweller on contract for specialty items, but you'd be surprised how many times we've found clones for so-called 'one-of-a-kind' pieces. We also have a specialist for children's toys, you see, not to make them, but to modify them. Children specialize their toys like no one else. A certain teddy bear is missing an eye, or an action figure has one black boot and one brown. Our special-ist, she has a warehouse in Lund. I've even seen it, a massive old airplane hangar, with nothing but specialty piles of exact toy pieces: dolls' hairbrushes and Action Man guns—hundreds of piles, thousands. Reminds me of when I visited Auschwitz as a student—the hills of eyeglasses and little children's shoes. I don't know how she does it, Ingvilde. She is driven.

I remember once we needed a 'special penny.' The client was specific. He used to be some kind of 'enter-tainment agent' in Hollywood, managed *name withheld for legal reasons* and a lot of other dead stars. In his letter he said that he once took his son to a place called

'Travel Town,' some sort of train museum in Los Angeles. He said it was the only time he'd ever spent a full afternoon with his son. Travel Town had one of those machines where you put a penny in, and cranking the handle presses it into a special medallion. The client had said that on the day they fled, his son had refused to leave it behind. He even made his father punch a hole through it so he could wear it around his neck on a shoelace. Half the client's letter was devoted to describing that special penny. Not just the design, but the colour, ageing, thickness, even the spot on it where he'd punched the hole. I knew we'd never find anything close to that. So did Ingvilde, but you know what she did? She made another one, completely identical. She found the company's records online and gave a copy of the design to a local machinist. She aged it like a master chemist—the right combination of salt, oxygen, and artificial sunlight. Most importantly, she made sure that the penny was made before the 1980s, before the American government removed most of the copper. You see, when you squeeze it flat and the inside metal shows... Sorry 'too much information' as you Americans say. I only mention it to illustrate the kind of dedication we have to our work here. Ingvilde, incidentally, works on a subsistence salary. She's like me—'rich person's guilt.'

We reach F deck, the deepest level aboard The African Queen. *Although artificially lit like the deck above, these bulbs are as bright as the prewar sun.* We try to simulate sunlight, *Kiersted explains,* and each compartment is specially equipped with sounds and smells tailored to the client. Most of the time it's peaceful— the smell of pine and the chirp of birds—but it really depends on the individual. We once had a man from mainland China, a test case, to see if it was worth their government setting up their own operation. He was from Chongqing, and he needed the sounds of traffic and the smells of industrial pollution. Our team actually had to mix up an audio file of specific Chinese cars and trucks, as well as this noxious brew of coal and sulphur and lead-filled gasoline.

It succeeded. Just like the special penny. It had to. Otherwise why the hell would we do it? Not just spend all the time and money, but the sanity of our workers.

Why are we constantly reliving something the whole bleeding world is trying to forget? Because it works. Because we help people, we give them exactly what the company name says. We have a seventy-four per cent success rate. Most of our clients are able to rebuild some semblance of a life, to move beyond their tragedy, obtain some semblance of 'closure.' That's the only reason you'd find someone like me here. This is the best place to work through 'rich person's guilt.'

We come to the last compartment. Kiersted reaches for his key, then turns to face me. You know, before the war, 'rich' used to mean material possessions—money, things. My parents didn't have either, even in a socialist country like Denmark. One of my friends was rich, always paid for everything, even though I never asked him to. He always felt guilty about his wealth, even admitted it to me once, about how 'unfair' it was that he had so much. 'Unfair.' *For the first time since our meeting, his smile fades.* I didn't lose one family member. I mean it. We *all* survived. I could figure out what was coming, as Americans say, 'put two and two together.' I knew enough to sell my house, buy the tools to survive, and get my family to Svalbard six months before the panic. My wife, our son, our two daughters, my brother, and his whole family—they're all still alive—with three grandchildren and five great nieces and nephews. My friend who had 'so much,' I treated him last month. They call it 'rich person's guilt,' because life is the new wealth. Maybe they should call it 'rich person's shame,' because, for some reason, people like us almost never talk about it. Not even to each other. One time I met with Ingvilde at her shop. She had a picture on her desk, facing away from me when I entered. I didn't knock, so I surprised her a little bit. She snapped that frame down on her desk before she even knew it was me. Instinct. Guilt. Shame. I didn't ask who was in the picture.

We stop at the final compartment. A clipboard rests on the bulkhead next to the hatch, a clipboard holding another legal disclaimer. Kiersted looks at it, then me, uncomfortably.

I apologize. I know you've already signed one, but because you're not an EU citizen, regulations demand that you reread and re-sign another form. The rereading part is a pain in the arse, and if it were up to me, I'd allow you to just sign it, but *His eyes flick to the surveillance camera on the overhead.*

I pretend to read. Kiersted sighs.

I know that a lot of people don't agree with what we do here. They think it's immoral, or at least wasteful. I understand. For a lot of them, not knowing is a gift. It protects them and drives them. They use it to push their lives forward, rebuild both physically and mentally, because they want to be ready for the day when that missing person suddenly walks through the door. For them, limbo is hope, and sometimes, closure is the death of hope.

But what about the other type of survivors, the ones who're paralyzed by limbo? These are the ones who search endlessly through ruins and mass graves and endless, endless lists. These are the survivors who've chosen truth over hope but can't move forward without some physical proof of that truth. Of course, what we provide isn't the truth, and they know it, deep down. But they believe it because they want to believe it, just like the ones who look into the void and see hope.

I finish filling out the last page of the form. Kiersted reaches for his key card.

Incidentally we've managed to assemble a basic psychological profile of those who seek our help. They tend to be of an aggressive nature—active, decisive, used to making their own destiny. *His eyes dart sideways to me.* This is a broad generalization, naturally, but for many of them, losing control was the worst part of that time, and this process is as much about regaining that control as it is about saying good-bye.

Kiersted slides his card, the lock flashes from red to green, and the door opens. The compartment I step into smells like sage and eucalyptus, and the sound of waves crashing echoes through bulkhead-mounted speakers. I stare at the subject in front of me. It stares back. It pulls at the restraints, trying to get to me. Its jaw drops open. It moans.

I am not sure how long I stare at the 'subject' in front of me. Eventually I turn to Kierstad, nod my approval, and notice the smile return to his face.

The Danish psychiatrist walks to a small locked cabinet on the rear bulkhead. 'I see you didn't bring your own.'

I shake my head.

Kiersted returns from the cabinet and places a small automatic pistol into my hand. He checks to make sure there is only one round in the chamber, then he steps back, exits the compartment, and closes the hatch behind me.

I centre the laser sight on the subject's forehead. It lunges at me, rasping and snapping. I pull the trigger.

Steve and Fred

'There's too many of them!' Naomi shrieked, the sound perfectly matching the skidding of the motorcycle's tyres.

They came to rest just short of the tree-line, the Buell's engine purring between their legs. Steve's eyes narrowed as he scanned the outer wall. It wasn't the zombies that bothered him. The lab's main gate was blocked. A Humvee had collided with the burned-out hulk of what looked like a semi's tractor. The trailer must have continued forward, turning over as it slammed into the two vehicles. Bright, ice-like pools shone where fire had melted parts of the aluminum walks. *Can't get in that way.* Steve glanced over his shoulder at Naomi. 'Time to use the service entrance.'

The neuroscientist actually cocked her head. 'There *is* one?'

Steve couldn't help but chuckle. For someone so smart, Naomi sure could be dumb. Steve licked his finger and placed it dramatically in the wind. 'Let's find out.'

The lab was completely surrounded. He'd expected that. There had to be, what, a few hundred shuffling and groping at each side of the hexagonal perimeter.

'I can't see another gate!' Naomi shouted over the bike's roar.

'We're not looking for one!' Steve shouted back.

There! A spot where the living dead had crowded against the wall. Maybe there had been something on the other side: a living survivor, a wounded animal, who knew, who cared. Whatever it was had been tasty enough to entice enough Stinkers to crush some of their buddies against the naked cinderblocks. The pressure had created a solid mass of compressed necrotic flesh, its shallow angle allowing the still-mobile Stinkers to literally walk up it and over the wall.

The 'ramping' must have happened at least a few hours ago. The original prey had long since been devoured. Only a few ghouls now stumbled or crawled over the undead ramp. Some of its parts still moved: a waving arm or a clicking jaw. Steve couldn't have cared less about them; it was the mobile ones still slouching over them he worried about. *Just a few*. He nodded imperceptibly. *No problem.*

Naomi didn't react when Steve aimed the bike's nose at the ramp. Only when he gunned the engine did she look straight ahead to his target.

'Are you—' she began.

'Only way in.'

'That's *crazy!*' she screamed, loosening her grip on his waist as if to leap off the Buell.

Steve's left hand instinctively shot out, holding her wrist and pulling it to him. Looking back at her terrified gaze, he flashed his signature grin. 'Trust me.'

Wide-eyed and chalk pale, Naomi could only nod and hug him with all her might. Steve turned back to the ramp, continuing to grin. *Okay, Gunny Toombs, this one's for you!*

The Buell took off like a rifle bullet, Hansen leaning into the howling wind. Five hundred yards... four hundred... three... Some of the zombies near the ramp began to notice them, turning and stumbling towards the oncoming crotch rocket. Two hundred yards... one hundred... and now they were massing, grouping into

37

a small but tight swarm blocking the ramp. Without flinching, Steve swung the M4 out of its worn leather scabbard and with eyes still fixed firmly ahead he bit down hard on the weapon's charging handle. It was a move he'd only tried once before, that night his Harrier had crashed outside Fallujah. The impact had broken one arm and both legs, but not his warrior's spirit. He'd tried using his teeth to cock the automatic carbine. It'd worked then, and damn if it worked now. The first round clicked reassuringly into the chamber.

No time to aim. He'd have to shoot from the hip. *Crack!* The closest one's left eye disappeared, a reddish brown cloud exploding out the back of its head. Steve might have commented on his marksmanship, if only there was time. *Crack! Crack!* Two more went down, falling like puppets with their strings cut. This time he smiled. *Still got it.*

The path began to open, but at the blinding speed they were traveling, would it open fast enough? 'Oh my god!' Naomi screamed.

With barely half a dozen bike lengths to go before they hit the ramp, Steve squeezed the M4's trigger, spraying a fully automatic burst of copper-coated tickets to hell. *Kiss Satan for me,* Steve thought. *Or my ex-wife, whichever you see first.*

The carbine clicked on empty just as the last zombie fell, and with a soft crunch and a bang, one hundred and forty-six horses thundered onto the ramp. With the Buell's wheels tearing up its putrid surface as they went, Steve and Naomi catapulted clear over the fence.

'OOOH-RAHH!' Steve shouted, and for just a split second, he was back in the cockpit, shrieking over the Iraqi desert, showering fire and death in a star spangled storm. Unlike the AV-8 jump jet, however, this machine couldn't be steered once airborne.

The Buell's front tyre smashed into the parking lot asphalt and skidded on a puddle of human remains. The impact catapulted both from the custom leather saddle. Steve tucked, rolled, and slammed against the tyre of a smashed Prius. The hybrid's driver, armless, faceless, stared down at him from the open driver's door. *Too bad the 'save the Earth' car couldn't do the same for its owner,* he thought.

Steve sprang to his feet. He could see Naomi lying

several yards away. She was face down, unmoving. *Shit.* The bike lay in the exact opposite direction. No way to tell if either of them was alive.

The moans and stench hit him like a one-two punch. He whirled just in time to see the first of the zombie horde begin to slouch towards them. Where the hell was the M4? He'd felt it slip from his grasp as they hit, heard it skitter across the hard surface. It must have gone under a car, but which one? There must have been several hundred vehicles still in the parking lot, which also meant that there must be several hundred undead former owners still on the grounds. No time to worry about that now, and no time to start looking for the weapon. The ghouls, about twenty of them now, advanced slowly towards Naomi's motionless body.

Steve's hand first went for the 9mm in his jacket. *No.* He stopped himself. If the M4 was damaged or lost, his Glock would be their only ballistic weapon. *Plus*, he thought, his finger's closing on familiar sharkskin hilt behind his back, *it just wouldn't be fair to Musashi.*

SSCHHIING! The ninjatô's twenty-three-inch

blade glinted in the noonday sun, as bright and clear as the day Sensei Yamamoto had presented it to him in Okinawa. 'Its name is Musashi,' the old man had explained. 'The Warrior Spirit. Once drawn, its thirst must be slaked with blood.' Well, he thought, let's hope that syrupy crap those Stinkers have in their veins counts.

A zombie loomed in the blade's reflection. Steve spun, catching it cleanly under the neck. Bone and muscle separated like ice under flame as the still snapping head rolled harmlessly under a torched minivan.

Ground and centre.

Another zombie reached out to grab Steve's collar. He ducked under its right arm and came up behind its back. Another head went rolling.

Breathe and strike.

A third took Musashi's blade right through its left eye.

Dodge and swing.

A fourth lost the top of its head. Steve now stood only a few paces from Naomi.

Ground and centre!

A fifth Stinker found its skull cleaved right down the middle.

'Steve.' Naomi looked up, voice weak, eyes unfocused. She was alive.

'I got ya, babe.' Steve yanked her to her feet, simultaneously slamming Musashi's blade through the ear of a ghoul slouching between them. He thought about trying to find the M4, but there just wasn't enough time. *Plenty more where we're going.*

'C'mon!' Steve pulled her through an encroaching swarm and together they ran to the overturned Buell. When he felt the engine roar beneath him—*Made in the USA!*—he wasn't surprised. Another roar could also be heard, dull and faint and growing with each passing second. Steve tilted his head to the smoke filled sky. There it was: their ride out of here, a small black speck set against the crimson sun.

'You call a cab?' Steve said, smiling at Naomi. For just the briefest of moments, the beautiful egghead smiled back.

They were only a hundred yards from the lab's open double doors. No problem there. Four flights of stairs. Steve patted the motorcycle. Again, no problem. 'We just gotta get to the heliport on the…' Steve trailed off. His eyes locked on someone—no, some*thing*. A ghoul was shuffling towards them from behind a smashed SUV. It was short and slow, and even on foot, he and Naomi could have left it in their dust. But Steve wasn't planning on leaving. Not just yet. 'Keep the engine running,' he said, and for once Naomi didn't question him.

Even with the rotted skin, the dried blood, the lifeless, milk-white eyes, she'd also recognized Theodor Schlozman. 'Go,' was all she said.

Steve dismounted the bike and walked slowly, almost casually over to the approaching ghoul.

'Hey, Doc,' he said softly, his voice cold as arctic death. 'Still tryin' to save Mother Earth from her spoiled children?'

Schlozman's jaw dropped slowly open. Broken, stained teeth poked through chunks of rotting human flesh. 'Huuuuuuuuuaaaaaaaa,' rasped the former Nobel prize-winner, his bloody hands reaching for Steve's throat.

The Marine let him get almost close enough to touch. 'As you used to say,' he smirked, 'arms are for hugging,' and swinging Musashi like an honour guard rifle he sliced off Schlozman's fingers, then hands, then forearms, before leaping into the air and smashing the paleoclimatologist's head sideways with a roundhouse kick.

The brain that had once been hailed as 'Evolution's Crowning Achievement' exploded from the shattered skull. Still intact, it went spinning towards the Buell, landing with a wet splat right at the base of the front tyre. *Touchdown.*

The Marine sheathed his assassin's short sword and walked slowly back to Naomi.

'We all done?' she asked.

Steve looked up at the approaching Blackhawk. Five minutes till they hit the roof. *Right on time.* 'Just had to take out the trash,' he answered without looking at her.

He gunned the engine and felt Naomi's arms grip him tightly around the waist. 'Back there,' she said, tilting her head to the spot where he'd rescued her, 'did you call me 'Babe'?'

Steve cocked his head in perfect innocence and spoke the only French he would ever want to learn: 'Moi?'

Steve gunned the engine and the brain of Professor Theodor Emile Schlozman splattered under spinning rubber like an overripe tomato. Steve smirked as the bike thundered towards…

Fred closed the book. He should have stopped several pages back. The pain behind his eyes had now spread to his forehead and down his neck. Most of the time he could ignore the constant headache. Most of the time it was just a dull pulse. The last few days though, it was getting almost debilitating.

He lay flat on his back, his skin sticking to the smooth granite floor. He rested his head on the oily, crusty rag that had once been his T-shirt and tried to focus on the centre of the ceiling. The light fixture above him almost looked like it was on. At this point in the afternoon, sunlight from the small window struck the bulb's prism glass bowl. Rainbow sparkles, dozens of them, marched beautifully across the cream-colored wallpaper. This was by far his favourite part of the day, and to think he hadn't even noticed it when he first arrived. *It's the only thing I'll miss when I get out of here.*

And then they were gone. The sun had moved.

He should have thought of that, planned better. If he'd known what time it was going to happen, he could have read up until then. He probably wouldn't have even gotten such a bad headache. He should have worn a watch. Why didn't he wear a watch? *Stupid.* His cell phone always had the time, and date, and... everything. Now his cell phone was dead. How long ago had that happened?

Way to be prepared, asshole.

Fred closed his eyes. He tried to massage his temples. Bad idea. The first upward motion tore the scabs between skin and fingernail stubs. The pain drew a quick hiss. *Fuckin' idiot!* He exhaled slowly, trying to calm himself. *Remember...*

His eyes flicked open. They swept the walls. *One hundred seventy-nine*, he counted. *One hundred and seventy-eight.* It still worked. *One hundred and seventy-seven.*

Counting… recounting, every bloody fist print, foot mark, panicked, frantic forehead indentation. *One hundred and seventy-six.*

This is what happens when you lose it. Do NOT go there again!

It always worked, although it always seemed to take a little bit longer. The last time he'd counted down to forty-one. This time was thirty-nine.

You deserve a drink.

Getting up was painful. His lower back ached. His knees ached. His thighs and calves and ankles burned a little bit. His head swam. That's why he'd given up morning stretches. Dizziness was worse than anything. That first time he'd shot up too quickly; the bruise on his face still throbbed from the fall. This time he thought he'd gotten up slowly enough. *Thought wrong, moron.* Fred dropped back to his knees. That was safer. He kept his head turned to the right; from this angle you *always* looked to the right! One hand on the rim to steady himself. The other dipped the plastic coke bottle into the reservoir. The water was only a few degrees colder, but was enough to jolt him back to full consciousness.

I need to drink more, not just for dehydration, but when I start to drift.

Four sips. He didn't want to overdo it. The plumbing was still on. For now. Better to conserve though. Better to be smart. His mouth was dry. He tried to swish. Another bad idea. All the pain washed over him at once; the cracks in his lips, the sores on his soft palate, the staph infection at the end of his tongue he'd gotten while unconsciously trying to suck out any last particles of food between his teeth. *Lotta fuckin' good that did.*

Fred shook his head in disgust. He wasn't thinking. He'd left his eyes open, and that's when he made the biggest mistake of the day. He looked left. His eyes locked on the floor-length mirror.

A sad little weakling stared back at him. Pale skin, matted hair and sunken, bloodshot eyes. He was naked. His janitor uniform didn't fit anymore. His body was living off its own fat.

Loser. No muscle, just fat.

Pussy. Hairy skin hung in blotched, deflated rolls.

Pathetic piece of shit!

Behind him, on the opposite wall, were the other marks he'd made. Day Two, when he'd stopped trying to widen the twelve-by-twelve-inch window with fingernails and teeth. Day Four, when he'd taken his last solid crap. Day Five, when he'd stopped screaming for help. Day Eight when he'd tried to eat his leather belt because he'd seen some Pilgrims do it in a movie. It was a nice thick belt, birthday present from—

No, don't go there.

Day Thirteen, when the vomiting and diarrhea had ended. What the hell was in that leather? Day Seventeen, when he became too weak to masturbate. And every day, filled with crying and begging, silent deals with God and whimpering calls for—

Don't.

Every day that ended, fittingly, huddled in the foetal position because there wasn't any room to stretch out.

DON'T THINK ABOUT HER!

But of course he did. He thought about her every day. He thought about her every minute. He talked to her in his dreams, and in the no-man's-land between dreams and reality.

She was okay. She *had* to be. She knew how to take care of herself. She was still taking care of him, wasn't she? That's why he was still living at home. He needed her, not the other way around. She would be fine. Of course she would.

He tried not to think about her, but he always did, and of course, the other thoughts always followed.

Failure! Didn't listen to the warnings! Didn't get out when you could!

Failure! Let yourself get trapped in this little room, not even the whole bathroom, just the closet-sized toilet box, drinking out of the goddamn shitter!

Failure! Didn't even have the fuckin' balls to break the mirror and do the honourable thing you should have done. And now if they get in, you don't even have the fuckin' strength!

Failure, FAILURE!

'FAILURE!'

He'd said that out loud. Fuck.

The loud thumping against the door sent him crumpling against the far corner. There were more of them; he could hear their moans echoing back down the hall. They matched those coming from the street below. They'd looked like an ocean down there, the last time he'd stood on the toilet to look. Nine floors down they roiled like a solid mass, stretching almost out of sight. The hotel must be entirely infested now, every floor, every room. The first week he'd heard shuffling through the ceiling above him. The first night, he'd heard the screams.

At least they didn't understand how to open a pocket door. He'd been lucky there: if it had been the kind of door that swung instead of slid shut; if the wood had been hollow instead of solid; if they'd been smart enough to figure out how to open it; if the doorway had been in the back of the outer bathroom, instead of off to the side…

The more the ones in the bedroom pushed, the more they pinned others in the bathroom helplessly against the rear wall. If it had been a straight line, their collective weight, their sheer numbers…

He was safe. They couldn't get in, no matter how much they clawed and struggled and moaned… and *moaned*. The toilet paper in his ears wasn't working as well anymore. Too much wax, too much oil had flattened them against the sides of the canals. If only he'd saved some more, and not tried to eat it.

Maybe its not the worst thing. He reassured himself, again. *When a rescue comes, you need to hear the chopper.*

It was better this way. When the moans got too bad, Fred reached for the book, one more bit of good luck he'd found by running in here. When he got out of here, he'd have to track down the original owner, somehow, and thank him for forgetting it next to the toilet. 'Dude, it totally kept me sane all that time!' he'd say. Well, maybe not quite like that. He'd rehearsed at least a hundred more eloquent speeches, all delivered over a couple of cool ones, or probably more likely a couple of MREs. That's what they'd been called on page 238: 'Meals Ready to Eat.' Did they really make them with chemical cookers right in the packaging? He'd have to go back and reread that part again. Tomorrow, though. Page 361 was his favourite; 361 to 379.

It was getting dark. He'd stop this time before his head hurt too much. Then maybe a few sips of water, and he'd make it an early night. Fred's thumb found the dog-eared page.

The Extinction Parade

We called them subdead, and to us, they were little more than a joke. They are so slow, and clumsy, and stupid. So stupid. We never considered them a threat. And why would we? They had existed beside us, beneath us rather, flaring up like brushfire since the first humanoids left the trees. Fanum Cocidi, Fiskurhofn, we had all heard the stories. One of us had even claimed to be present at Castra Regina, although we mainly considered him a braggart. Through the ages we had witnessed their bumbling eruptions and humanities' equally bumbling response. They had never been a serious threat, either to us or the solbreeders they devoured. They had always been a joke. And so I laughed again when I heard of a small outbreak in Kampong Raja. Laila had told me about it, on that warm, still night ten years ago.

'This isn't the first time. Not just this year, I mean.' Her tone was mildly fascinated, as if discussing any other rare natural phenomenon. 'Others have been talking, about Thailand, and Cambodia, maybe as far as Burma.' Again, I laughed, and perhaps said something disparaging about humans, probably wondering how long it would take them to clean up the mess. I didn't think about it again until a few months later. The whispers hadn't abated. We were entertaining Anson, a visitor from Australia. He'd come for the 'sport' as he called it, a chance to 'take in the local flavours'. We were both very taken with Anson, he was tall and beauteous and very, very young. He could not remember a time a before voice-wires and metal kites. His unburdened eyes glittered with envious vim.

'They've made it to Oz,' he said with childlike excitement. We were standing on our balcony, watching the Hari Merdeka fireworks blossom over the Petronas Towers. 'Isn't that amazing?' he marvelled, and both of us believed he meant the fireworks. 'At first I thought they could swim, they can, you know, not in the traditional sense more like waddling under water. But that's not how they ended up in Queensland. Something about illegal boat people. Nasty business, I hear, all covered up and so forth. I wish I'd had a chance to see some of them! I never have, you know, not 'in the flesh'.'

'Let's go tonight!' Laila chimed in suddenly. I could see that our guest's enthusiasm had infected her. I started to respond about the distance before dawn, before she cut me off with, 'No, not there. Right here, tonight! I hear there's a new flare up just a few hours away near Jerantut. We may have to trek into the bush a ways, but won't that be half the fun?' I was curious I admit. Months of rumours and a lifetime of stories had taken their toll. I confessed to them, as I confess to myself now, that I did in fact want to see one 'in the flesh'.

It is easy to forget, when you are one of us, how fast the rest of world can move. So much jungle had vanished, in what seemed the blink of an eye, replaced by motorways, tract housing, and mile after mile of palm oil plantations. 'Progress', 'Development': only last night, it seemed, Laila and I were haunting the rough, unlit streets of a new tin mining town called Kuala Lumpur. And to think I had followed her from Singapore because our previous home had become too 'civilized'. Now, as our Lexus LSA sped down a river of asphalt and artificial daylight.

We were not expecting the police roadblock and the police were not expecting us. They did not ask where we were going, or check our identification, or even point out that we had illegally crammed three riders into a two-seat motorcar. He just waved us away, one white-gloved hand pointing down the way we had come, while the other rested shakily on the flap of his holster. I will never forget his scent, or the scent of the other policemen behind him, or of the platoon of soldiers behind them. I had not smelled such concentrated fear since the '69 race riots. (Oh, what a glorious time that had been.) I could see on Laila's face how badly she wanted to return to the roadblock after our adventure. She must have seen the same look in me. 'Careful', she whispered, as one finger playfully poked my ribs. 'It's not safe to drive drunk.'

We noticed the second smell several minutes later, after pulling off the motorway and returning to the site across the tops of trees. The olfactory impact struck us like a wall, human terror mixed with decaying flesh. A split second later, our ears were assailed with distant gunfire.

The neighbourhood must have been especially built for the plantation workers. Rows of neat little houses lined broad, newly paved streets. We could see shops, cafeterias, a pair of grade schools and the large Catholic church, now common for our country's Filipino guest workers. From the top of the church steeple, the highest point in this prefabricated settlement, I could only gawk at the carnage below. The fires caught my attention first, then the blood stains, then the drag marks, then the bullet holes lining several of the houses, many of which looked like their windows and doors had been stoved in by a mob. I noticed the bodies last, perhaps because they'd already cooled. Most of them were lying in pieces, a mélange of limbs, and torsos amongst loose organs and amorphous chunks of flesh. Some corpses remained reasonably intact, and I noticed all had small round holes in the centre of their heads. I reached over to point them out to Laila and noticed that both she and Anson had vacated our rooftop perch. I guessed they must have made for the sounds of shooting.

For a second I became lost in memory, lulled into nostalgia by the sensory banquet of collective human death. For a moment it was the 1950s again and I was lurking through the jungles in search of human prey. Laila and I still talked fondly of 'The Emergency', how we hunted the scent trails of either communist insurgents or commonwealth commandos, how we struck from the shadows while our quarry's weapons (and bowels) discharged from panic, how we greedily supped upon the last succulent drops from their frantically beating hearts. 'If only' we would lament for decades, 'if The Emergency had lasted'.

I have heard it said that the more memories one acquires, the less room the mind has for conscious thought. I cannot speak for others, but at my age, after the remembrance of so many lifetimes crammed into my ancient skull, I do suffer from occasional lapses of 'preoccupation'. It was one of those lapses, lost in the recent past, and unconsciously licking my lips, that I descended from my omniscient perch, rounded the church's corner and practically collided with one of them. It was a man, or had been one recently. The right

side of his body was still smooth and supple. The left
side had been badly charred. Dark, viscous fluid oozed
from numerous, steaming wounds. The left arm below
the elbow had been severed, cleanly, as if from a
machine, or more probably, from one of those great
hacking knives the workers used to harvest their crops.
His left leg dragged slightly, digging a shallow trench
behind him. As he lunged forward, I instinctively drew
back, crouching for a lethal blow.

And then came the unexpected. He, it, just
slouched slowly right past me. It did not turn in my
direction. Its one good eye did not even make contact
with mine. I waved my hand in front of its face. Nothing. I stepped beside it and kept pace for several
seconds. Nothing. I even went so far as to stand directly
in front of it. Not only did the silent brute refuse to halt,
but it barrelled into me without even raising its arms.
Hitting the sidewalk, I let out an unexpected guffaw as
the subdead abomination trod over my body without
even taking notice!

Later I realized how foolish I had been to expect
any other reaction. Why should it have recognized me?

Was I food? Was I even 'alive' in the human sense? These creatures obeyed only their biological imperative, and that imperative drove them to seek out only 'living' beings. To its primitive, diseased brain I was practically invisible, an obstacle to be ignored and, at best, avoided. For a second I could only marvel at the absurdity of my situation, giggling like a child as this pathetic obscenity dragged its mangled carcass past me. Then rising to my feet, I withdrew my right arm and swung. I giggled again as the head tore easily from the shoulders, bounced hard against the opposite house, and came to rest at my feet. Its one working eye continued to move, continued to search and, ridiculously, continued to ignore me. That was the first time I came face to face with what the human solbreeders referred to as a 'zombie'.

The following months could be called 'the nights of denial'. They were the business as usual nights where we tried to ignore the threat growing steadily around us. We talked, or thought, very little about the subdead, and could not be bothered to keep abreast of the news. There were many stories, from both humans and our kind, of subdead risings on every continent. The subdeads were incessant and expanding, but most of all, they were just boring. We always seemed to be bored, such is the price of conditional immortality. 'Yes, yes, I've heard about Paris, and your point being?' 'Of course I know about Mexico City, who doesn't?' 'Oh for Hell's sake are we going to bring up Moscow again?' For three years we shut our eyes, as the crisis deepened and the humans continued to either die, or turn.

And in the fourth year, 'The Nights of Denial' became what we, ironically called, 'The Nights of Glory'. That was when general knowledge of the outbreak swept the world, when governments began formally revealing the nature of the crisis to their people. That was when global systems began to erode, when national links closed and national borders collapsed, when minor wars ignited and major riots raged across the world. That was when our kind entered a phase of unbridled, celebratory ecstasy.

For decades we had complained about the oppressive interconnection of the solbreeders. Railroads and electricity had placed enough pressure on our rapacious nature, to say nothing of the telegraph and the accursed telephone! Recently however, with the rise of both terrorism and telecommunications, it seemed as if every wall was now made of glass. As we'd once left Singapore, now Laila and I had recently been considering moving from the Malay Peninsula altogether. We'd discussed Sarawak or perhaps even Sumatra, anywhere the lights of knowledge hadn't yet burned away our dark corners of freedom. Now our exodus seemed unnecessary, as those lights began thankfully dimming.

For the first time in years, we could hunt without fear of cellphones or surveillance cameras. We could hunt in packs, and even linger over our struggling repasts. 'I'd almost forgotten what pure night looks like,' Laila had once gushed during a blackout hunt, 'oh what a delicious seasoning is chaos.' Those nights still found us deeply grateful for the subdead, and the liberating distraction they wrought.

One memorable night found Laila and I scaling the balconies of the Coronade Hotel. Below us, on Sultan Ismail Street, government troops thrust lances of tracer fire towards a horde of approaching cadavers. It was an intriguing spectacle, so much concentrated military might; grinding, pounding, pulverizing, yet still not eradicating the subdead. At one point we were forced to leap to the flat roof portion of the Sugei Wang Plaza (no small feat), as the shockwave of an aerial bomb brought a rain of glass from the hotel's windows. It was a fortuitous decision, because the Plaza's roof happened to be crammed with several hundred refugees. I gathered, from the opened food containers and dry water bottles, that the poor wretches must have been trapped there for some time. They smelled unwashed and exhausted, and so deeply, seductively afraid.

I remember little else, save flashes of violence and the backs of fleeing prey. I remember the girl, however. She must have been from the countryside, so many were flooding the cities in those days. Did her parents believe they were seeking shelter? Did she even have parents anymore? Her scent lacked none of the modern urban dwellers impurities, no ingested hormones or intoxicants, or even the cumulative stench of pollution. I relished her delectable purity, and later cursed myself for lingering with anticipation. She jumped without hesitation, without so much as a yelp. I watched per plunge directly into the groaning, writhing horde.

The subdead moved like a machine, a slow, deliberate mechanism with the sole purpose of transforming a shrieking human child into a mass of unrecognizable pulp. I remember her chest heaving its last breath, her eyes staring up at me with a last twinkle of recognition, before they were extinguished in a sea of hands and teeth.

In my youth I'd listened to an old occidental reminisce about the fall of Western Rome, and gnashed my teeth with envy at his experience of that empire's demise. 'Half a civilization burned,' he boasted, 'half a continent submerged in a millennium of anarchy.' I would salivate, literally, at his stories of hunting the lawless lands of Europe. 'It was liberation the likes you Asian's have never, and I fear, will never see!' How solid his prediction had seemed that short decade ago. Now it rang as hollow as the shell of our crumbling society.

I am not sure when ecstasy gave way to anxiety. It would be difficult to trace that exact moment. For me, personally, it came from Ngyuen, an old friend from Singapore. Both highly educated and naturally intelligent, he was Vietnamese by descent and had spent enough time in Paris to become a student of French existentialism. This might explain why he never succumbed to the capricious pleasure-seeking so common for our race. It might also explain why he was, to my knowledge, the first to sound the alarm.

We had met in Penang. Laila and I had been forced to vacate KL when an unchecked, daylight fire threatened to engulf our entire block. Several of our kind had recently been lost that way. We hadn't fully understood how comfortable our life had become in recent times, constricted yes, but also extremely comfortable. Most of us had long abandoned the notion of fortified nests. They had gone the way of the torch and the pitchfork. Most of us now lived as solbreeders, in comfortable and, in some cases, opulent urban palaces.

Anson had lived in one of those palaces, in a glittering tower far above Sydney harbour. Like the rest of our world, his city had degenerated into subdead induced bedlam. Like the rest of our race, his appetite had succumbed to bloody bacchanalian bliss. From what we heard he had retired one morning to his high rise alcazar, just as the Australian government gave permission to use military force. No one is sure how his building collapsed. We'd heard theories ranging from stray artillery fire, to demolitions detonated far beneath the city streets. We hoped that poor Anson had been atomized in the explosion, or else quickly immolated in morning sun. We shunned the image of him pinned beneath thousands of tons of debris, tortured by pin-pricks of sunlight as his life force slowly drained away.

Nguyen had almost suffered a similar fate. He had had the good sense to flee Singapore the night before a solbreeder offensive. That evening he had watched from across the Johor Straits as his homeland of over three centuries burned. He had also had the presence of mind to bypass the crucible of KL and make his way to the new solbreeder 'Security Zone' of Penang. Millions of refugees were inundating the several hundred square kilometres of urbanized coastline. With them trickled dozens of our kind, some from as far away as Dhaka. We had managed to 'acquire' several restricted domiciles of our own, removing the previous human owners and guarding against future squatters. What our new homes lacked in comfort they made up for in security. At least, that is what we told ourselves as the situation deteriorated and swarms of subdead moved steadily closer to Penang. It was in one of these domiciles, after a night of hunting the nearby refugee camps, that Nguyen first voiced his concern.

'I've done the math,' he said anxiously, 'my calculations are disturbing.' At first I didn't know what he was talking about. The older generation have deplorable social skills. The more they retreated into their memories, the harder it was to communicate. 'Famine, disease, suicide, interspecies murder, combat casualties and, of course, subdead infection.' My puzzled expression must have been obvious. 'The humans!' He hissed impatiently at me. 'We're losing them! The slouching filth is slowly exterminating them.'

Laila laughed. 'They've always been trying to do that, and humans have always put them down.'

Nguyen shook his head angrily. 'Not this time! Not in this shrunken world we live in. There were more humans than there had ever been! There were travel and trade networks that linked these humans as never before! That's how the plague spread so rapidly and so far! The humans have created a world of historic contradictions. They have been erasing physical distances while at the same time erecting social-emotional ones.' He sighed angrily at our blank expressions. 'The more humans have extended their reach across the planet, the more they desired to withdraw within themselves. As the shrinking world created a higher level of material prosperity, they have used that prosperity to insulate themselves from one another. That is why, when the plague began to spread, there was no global, or even national call to arms! That is why governments worked in relative secret, and in vain, while their populations busied themselves with petty personal concerns! The average solbreeder didn't see what was happening until it was too late! And it is ALMOST too late! I've done the math! The homo sapiens are close to their sustainable tipping point. Soon there's going to be more subdead than living humans!'

'And so what?' I'll never forget those words, or the

casual, inconvenienced way Laila sighed them. 'So what if there'll be a few less solbreeders? Like you said, if they're too selfish and stupid to stop the subdead from hunting them, then why the hell should we care?'

Nguyen looked as if the sun had risen in Laila's eyes. 'You don't get it,' he rasped. 'You really haven't made the connection.' He paused for a second, retreating several steps and searching the room as if he'd dropped the right words somewhere on the carpet. 'We're not talking about 'a few less solbreeders', we're talking about all of them! ALL OF THEM!'

Now the entire room turned in Nguyen's direction, although his burning, accusing eyes stabbed directly into Laila's. 'The sapiens are fighting for their very survival! And they are losing!' He then spread his arms dramatically, drawing a semicircle of emptiness. 'And when the last one of them vanishes, what in hell's name are you or I or any of our race going to live on!?!?' Silence answered Nguyen. His eyes swept the assembled group. 'Have none of you thought beyond tonight's feeding? Do any of you comprehend what it means to have another organism compete with us for our one and only source of food!??!'

At that point I ventured a timid response, something on the order of 'but the subdead have to stop eventually. They have to know…'

'They don't know ANYTHING!' Nguyen cut me off. 'And you KNOW that! You KNOW the difference between their kind and ours! We hunt humans! They consume humanity! We are predators! They are a plague! Predators know not to overhunt, or overpopulate! We know to always leave one egg in the nest! We know that survival depends on maintaining the balance between ourselves and our prey! A disease doesn't know that! A disease will grow and grow until it's infected the entire host! And if killing that host means killing itself in the process, so be it! A disease has no concept of restraint or notion of tomorrow! It cannot grasp the long term consequences of its actions, and neither can the subdead! We can! But we don't! We've been condoning it! We've been CELEBRATING it! For the last few years we've been blithely dancing in a parade to our own extinction!

I could see that Laila was becoming agitated. Her eyes locked on Nguyen with a predatory gaze while her thin lips curled back around her fangs. 'There will be more solbreeders,' she said in a soft, almost hissing voice, 'there will always be more!'

And that became the conventional wisdom. From the historical, 'when have humans not risen to the challenge of the subdead?' to the pragmatic, 'yes, the present global human socioeconomic system might disintegrate but not the humans themselves' or the humorous, 'as long as humans keep fornicating with abandon, there will always be more'. From the dismissive to the confrontational, so many of our people clung to the same desperate argument, 'there will always be more'. Desperate is the only adjective that describes this new phase of our existence. As the subdead continued to multiply, as they surged over one human stronghold after another, the argument of 'there will always be more' became more insistent, more dogmatic, more desperate.

And yet it was not the disciples of 'more' that troubled my daylight sleep so deeply. It was those who thought as I did, who began to follow Nguyen's logic and 'do the math' for themselves. Humanity was indeed reaching its collective tipping point. The subdead had sparked a chain reaction, just as our Vietnamese sage had predicted. Every night the corpses stacked higher in Penang's streets and hospitals and makeshift refugee camps. Malnutrition, sickness, suicide, and murder followed, and the subdead had not even reached our zone.

We knew there would not, could not 'always be more,' but then what was to be done? 'To be done'; the question at first seemed so alien. I could barely ask myself, let alone query others. Now that we were facing an apocalyptic threat, wouldn't the logical conclusion be to prevent it? Of course it would for anyone but a race of passive parasites.

We were like fleas watching our host dog fight for its life, never considering that we might have the power to aid it. We had always looked down on solbreeders as a so-called 'inferior race'. And yet that race, confronted daily with its own weakness and mortality, had taken destiny by the throat. While we skulked in the shadows, they had studied and sweated and changed the face of their world. And it was their world, not ours. We'd never felt any ownership of our 'host' civilization, no need to contribute, and hell forbid, fight for it in any way. While the great metamorphoses, the wars and migrations and epic revolutions, passed before our eyes, we craved only blood and safety and habitual relief from ennui. Now, as the course of history threatened to carry us into the abyss, we remained shackled by near genetic paralysis.

These revelations are, naturally, the harvest of hindsight. They were not so lucid as I stalked my hunting ground that night at Temenggor lake. The human barricade in the 4 Motorway was their latest breakwater against the surging tide of subdead. What was left of the military garrison had erected some makeshift fortifications but refrained from destroying the bridge. They must have still clung to the idea of reclaiming the far bank. The central island was designated as a 'quarantine' zone, the former nature preserve now overrun with 'detainees'. Our kind found it to be the ideal location for stalking some unsuspecting refugee who'd strayed too far from the others. That night ran red with gluttony. I had already fed on two previous refugees before purging my body and searching for a third. Such acts had previously been unheard of among our people, now it was becoming commonplace. Perhaps it was some misguided means of overcompensation, an unconscious need to exert control over our situation. I am still uncertain of the deeper motives. From a conscious, emotional perspective, I can claim all trace of enjoyment had evaporated from my hunts. Now rage was all I felt for my victims, rage and irrational contempt. My kills were becoming unnecessarily painful. I found myself mutilating my victims' bodies, even taunting them in the moment before death.

I once went so far as to cripple the target with a blow to the head, but left him conscious enough to hear my words. 'Why don't you do something?' I mocked, my face inches from his. He was old and foreign and could not understand my language. 'Go ahead!' I snarled, 'Do something!' It became a psychotic mantra, 'Do something, do something, DO SOMETHING!' Recalling it now, I suspect 'Do something' was less a provocation, than a masked cry for help. 'Please do something' was what I should have said, 'Your species has the tools and the will! Please do something! Find a solution that will save both our races! Please do something! While there's enough of you! While there's still time! Do something! DO SOMETHING!'

That night by Temenggor lake, I was too blood drunk to commit such acts on my latest feast. The haggard wretch was equally incapacitated, only her condition was mental. Many of the refugees were suffering from what the humans referred to as 'shell shock'. Many of their bodies had survived beyond their minds' limitations. The horrors they witnessed, the losses they endured, many of their psyches had simply melted into oblivion. The woman I fed on had as much recognition of my presence as the subdead. As I opened her veins, she gave what could only have been a small sigh of relief.

I remember how repulsive her blood had tasted on my tongue, thin and starving and tainted with the cumulative residue released from self-digested cellulite. I considered rejecting her mid-consumption and searching for a fourth victim. Suddenly I became distracted by a cacophony of screams and moans, louder than before, and coming from the western side of the bridge.

The subdead had broken through. I saw it the moment I stepped out of the jungle. The human barrier of overturned cars and debris was swarming with carnivorous automatons. Whether the defenders had run short of bullets or courage, I did not know. All I saw were humans in full retreat before the swarm. Hundreds, perhaps thousands of the creatures surged over the barricade, crushing their brethren that had formed a ramp of compressed flesh.

I sprang up onto the bridge, calling for Laila in the pitch only detectable by our species. No answer came. I scanned the fleeing human multitude, hoping to discern her deep amber aura against bright pink human mob. Nothing. She was gone, nothing but the frantic solbreeders and the surging, howling subdead. That was the first time I felt it, an emotion so powerful and so long forgotten. It was not anxiety, I had become all too familiar with that sensation. Anxiety is the fruit of potential harm; fire or sunlight, or a new substrain of biomechanical doom. This was not anxiety. This was not conscious thought. This was primal and instinctual and it gripped me like an invisible claw. This was something I had not felt since my heart had stopped beating so many centuries ago. This was a human emotion. This was fear.

It is a curious thing to be a spectator to your own actions. I remember every tear, every punch, every second of violence as I tore into the subdead horde. Ten, eleven, twelve skulls imploding, necks cleaving… Fifty-seven, fifty-eight spines shattering, brains rupturing, one hundred and forty-five, one hundred and forty-six… I counted each one, as the hours stretched and corpses mounted. Driven was the only word that describes my actions that night, operating without will, as a daybreeder would one of their great machines. Driven without inhibition or pause, until another hand grasped mine. I recoiled, drawing to strike, and found my eyes staring into Laila's.

Her hands were shaking, slick and black with subdead putrefaction. Her eyes burned with animal exhilaration. 'Look!' she growled, referring to the hundreds of silent, mutilated mounds before us. Nothing stirred, save a few severed, snapping heads. Laila lifted her foot above one of the air-gnawing skulls and brought it down with a guttural grunt. 'We did this,' she exclaimed, the realization mounting within both our chests, 'WE did this!' Panting for the first time in centuries, she waved her hand over the distant barricade, and the next wave of subdead now traversing it. 'More.' Her whispers grew into roars, 'More. More! MORE!'

We lay dying for the next few days. How could we have known that subdead fluid was so lethal. The micro fissures of close combat, the deep immersion in their virulent corruption. After a night of over a thousand slain, we appeared destined to be the final casualties. 'At least you fed before,' said Nguyen, as he came to our darkened sanctuary. 'I have discovered the sapiens' blood is the only antidote to your contamination.' He had brought with him two meals, a male and a female, both bound and struggling and screaming against their gags. 'I considered silencing them,' he said, 'but I chose purity over convenience.' He then held the females' neck to my lips. 'The influx of adrenaline will only hasten your recovery.'

'Why?' I asked, surprised at Nguyen's generosity. Selfishness was a common trait among our people, both in material possessions and blood. 'Why save these morsels for us? Why not…'

'You're both famous,' he announced with almost youthful giddiness, 'What you did on the bridge, what both of you accomplished… you've inspired our race!'

I could see Laila's eyes widen as she greedily fed on the male. Before either of us could speak, Nguyen continued with, 'Well, you've inspired our race in Penang. Who knows what anyone of either species is doing outside this safe zone. But we'll sort that out later. Right now the critical fact is that you showed us what is possible! You showed us a solution, an escape! Now we can all strike back together! Some others have already started! These past three nights at least a dozen have leapt beyond the human defences, and have penetrated deep into the heart of the approaching mega swarms. Thousands of subdead have fallen! Millions more will follow!'

I don't know if it was Nguyen's words or the rush of human blood, but my thoughts sank quickly into numbing euphoria.

'You saved us!' he cooed in both our ears. 'You have declared war.'

And the war began with many of our kind following the example that Laila and I had set on Lake Temmengor. At least we had learned from our near fatal mistake of exposure, and either sheathed our hands in gloves or else bound them with impermeable material. Some of our kind learned to fight entirely with their feet, developing what I suppose the solbreeders call a 'martial art'. These 'skull dancers' carried themselves high above the flailing arms of the subdead, leaping and crushing as if on a sea of eggshells. It was graceful and deadly and while not particularly important to our war effort, it was also one of the few aspects of our culture that anyone could claim was truly ours.

Unfortunately every skull dancer was matched by an equal number of 'emulators', those of our kind who chose to arm themselves as solbreeders. The emulators wielded human inventions; firearms, blades or bludgeons. Their argument being that such implements were more 'efficient' than our bare bodies. Many chose their weapons based on the era, or the geography of their previous lives. It was not uncommon to see former Chinese brandishing a broad, double handed dadao or former Malay carrying the traditional Keris Sundang. One night in the Cameron Highlands, I actually observed a former occidental rapidly firing and reloading a rusted 'Brown Bess' flintlock musket. 'Some talk of Alexander, and some of Hercules', he sang with motions so quick they matched the speed of a modern day automatic rifle, 'of Hector and Lysander and such great names as these!' As impressive as the spectacle was, I could only wonder at his remaining supply of powder and shot. Where on Earth had he acquired either? For that matter where did any of them attain their particular implements, and how much time did they waste attaining them? How truly 'efficient', or simply some subconscious emotional need to reconnect with the proactive hearts that once beat within them?

I believe the latter lay at the centre of another, even more fanatical emulator clique. We dubbed these imbeciles the 'militarized emulators' as they organized themselves into quasi-human 'strike teams'. They bestowed ranks and designations upon themselves, even creating protocol such as salutes and secure passwords. Within a month, several of these 'strike teams' had sprouted in and around Penang.

The most notable was 'Field Marshal Peng' (not his real name) and his 'Army of the Blood Line.'

'The plan for victory is being finalized as we speak,' he told me one night while gesturing to a map of Southeast Asia. Laila and I had been curious enough to pay a visit to the 'Field Marshal', hoping that he might very well have the answer to our precarious predicament. Twenty minutes at 'SAC HQ' cured us of that hope. From what we could tell, the army consisted of half a dozen members, all clustered around a collection of human maps and human satellite radios and human books on everything military. They all looked quite resplendent in their gold-trimmed, black uniforms, complete with blood red berets and even matching human, and I write this without jest, sunglasses. More impressive than their appearance were their proficient debating skills. 'Static Defence', 'Choke Point', 'Search and Destroy,' and 'Clear, Hold and Build', were just a few of the terms we caught amidst the flurry of verbal clashes. The 'Marshal' must have noticed our glances over his shoulder, and our reactions to his 'Strategic Operations Staff'.

'The final blow needs to be decisive,' he said confidently, smiling and nodding in his staff's direction. 'Therefore, let a hundred flowers bloom. Let a hundred schools contend.'

'If only we had a hundred of anything,' sighed Laila as we dismissed the 'Army of the Blood Line' and the 'Bare Fang Militia', and the 'Noctactical Wing' and the handful of other militarized emulator bands who barely stopped a few raindrops of the raging subdead storm.

Numbers continued to be our enemies' greatest asset, numbers in both bodies and hours. How many of the latter found our kind feeding, resting, or just cowering from the rays of the sun? Could any of this be said for the other side? As we retreated with each sunrise, those decaying carcasses continued to advance, kill and multiply. For every swarm we obliterated, the following night saw instant replacements. For every kilometre we cleansed in darkness, the new light brought renewed infestation. Despite all our vaunted physical strengths, despite our supposed 'superior' intelligence, despite the overwhelming advantage of not even being noticed by our adversaries, we fought as hapless gardeners in the face of an overwhelming blight.

One faction might have been able to improve our situation, and they called themselves the Sirenes. These courageous individuals took it upon themselves to seek out our kind all over the world, and rally them to Penang for the sake of a coordinated effort. The Sirenes believed that only a true army of our kind, massing in the hundreds and concentrating at one specific location, could eventually begin to purge our planet. I applauded their efforts, but had little confidence in their success. With the breakdown of global transport, how were any us going to travel farther than a few dozen, or perhaps hundred miles before the next dawn? Even if they found shelter from the sun each morning, could the same be said for nourishment? Could they really be expected to 'live off the land', hoping to stumble upon some isolated human outpost every night? Even if some Sirenes succeeded in contacting more of us, how could they convince them that Penang was any safer than their present location? How was a mass exodus to Penang even possible? One of our kind trekking across the globe was next to impossible. How could a supposed 'Army'? Against all logic, I never lost hope that one night would see a ship appear off our cost, or an aircraft (as if any of us ever learned to fly) suddenly swoop out of the sky. Through all my nights of combat, I continued to fantasize that suddenly hundreds of us would suddenly materialize out of the night. I had seen similar scenes from human history, places like Stalingrad and the Elbe River, images of handshakes and embraces, icons of renewed hope and ultimate victory. These icons haunted my fitful rest, tantalizing and tormenting as I waited in vain for the Sirenes.

There were other possibilities, options that might have meant our salvation but only at the cost of sacrilege. Our race had no 'religion' in the spiritual, daybreeder sense of the word. Similarly we carried no complex code of moral conduct. Our allegiance lay in only two inviolate taboos.

The first was to create only one other in our own image. It was the reason time had failed to expand our population. While never discussed, this silent commandment must have had its roots in the predator's notion of balance. As Nguyen had said, it would have been impossible to leave one egg in the nest if too many predators walked the earth. It was logical and reasonable, and the rise of the subdead, in fact, affirmed that notion of balance. But when faced with impending triumph of the subdead, could we have not, perhaps this once, slightly modifies our ancient cannon?

There were perhaps a hundred of us in Penang, the greatest concentration of our kind in history. Of that figure, perhaps a quarter departed the zone as Sirenes, while another quarter elected for feckless militaristic masturbation. That left fifty true combatants capable of fighting for only a few short hours each night before hunger, fatigue, and the eventual dawn forced withdrawal. While our nightly kills numbered in the thousands, they still had left a propogating force of millions.

We might have corrected that equation with just the right amount of transformed solbreeders. We could have chosen carefully and prudently, adding just enough reinforcements without upsetting the balance between pack and herd. We might have created a force large enough to clear the Malay Peninsula, then Southeast Asia, and from there, who knows? We might have given the humans just the kind of breathing room they needed, enough time to possibly pool enough resources to finish purging the planet without our assistance. The opportunity lay within our grasp, and yet none of us ever considered seizing it.

Likewise our second precept remained beyond discussion; direct open contact with humanity. Like recruitment, anonymity found its roots in the logical desire for survival. How could we, as predators, reveal ourselves to our prey? Did we desire the same fate as the sabre tooth cat, the short faced bear, or a host of other apex killers who had once feasted upon human bones? Throughout human history, our existence remained relegated to myths and childhood parables. Even now, in the midst of our parallel struggle for existence, we strove to conceal our efforts from solbreeder eyes.

What if we had abandoned the charade, and revealed ourselves to our unwary allies? Full disclosure would not have been necessary. We might have bypassed the ignorant masses in favour of an enlightened few. If not the Malaysian government then perhaps others operating 'in exile' throughout the region. There must have still been some nearby safe zones like ours, some human leaders who were willing to come to a mutual understanding. We would not have asked much, just the right to continue hunting as before. Homosapien leaders had never been loath to sacrifice their own people. We might have even negotiated distinct boundaries, feeding off specific refugees who'd lost everything in the maelstrom. Who would mourn, or even notice their passing? Perhaps the more lucid might have even submitted themselves willingly. Self-sacrifice was nothing new to solbreeders. Some might have actually prided themselves on literally spilling their blood for the survival of their species. Would it have been such a high price for their race to consider? Would it have been such a high risk for our race to propose? As with recruitment, I have no knowledge of any challenge to this sacrosanct law. It is bitter consolation that cowardice is not just a vulnerability of our species. In my short life, I have seen too many hearts of both night and day that lacked the simple courage to question their convictions. I now count myself among the guilty, who chose certain oblivion over opaque prospect of 'Why Not?'

My sleep was dreamless the day Perai fell. It was the largest concentration of refugee camps in the Penang security zone, which was why some of us had set up residence just across the river in Butterworth. It was still relatively easy to feed in the mainland safe zone, unlike Penang Island where the government was able to enforce marshal law. Perai's crimson fountain fortified us every night for battle. It also fortified the human effort as the last manufacturing base for munitions.

When the explosion occurred, I was resting deeply after our most ferocious battle to date. Three dozen of us had crept stealthily over the daybreeder wall along the narrow Juru river and attacked the heart of a swarm roiling out of Tok Panjang. We had returned depleted and discouraged, barely blunting their incessant push towards the humans. From our commandeered, thin walled flat, we could hear the collective moans rising with the morning breeze.

'Tomorrow night will be different,' Laila assured me. 'The solbreeders still have the Juru as a natural barrier and every day they build their wall just a little bit higher.' I wasn't sure if I believed her, but I was too fatigued to argue. We collapsed in each other's arms as dawn broke over the closing menace.

I awoke in mid-air, as the shock wave hurled me against the bedroom's far wall. A half second later I felt as if scores of white hot branding irons were suddenly pressed against my skin. The detonation had blown out our windows and the glass had shredded our blackout curtains. Still blind from the reflected daylight and gasping from my smoking wounds, I rolled to the floor while reaching frantically for Laila. Her arms found me first, reaching around my waist and pulling me over her shoulder. 'Don't struggle!' she shouted and threw a daycloak over my head. A leap, a crash of glass, and then we were on the concrete six stories down. Laila took off at a lightning dash, her steps echoing across a sea of shards. 'What...' I managed to croak.

'The factories!' Laila answered, 'A fire and accident... they're here! They're everywhere!'

I could smell her burning flesh. How much of her body was exposed? How much longer did she have before combusting? Those three seconds seemed a lifetime before I felt her leap again. Laila's grasp abruptly weakened as a cold, hard splash separated us.

The cloak floated from my face. What had been small, searing wounds now melted into a general, boiling torment. I could see that Laila had taken us into the Mallaca straight, and she was now leading me by the hand towards the pockets of shade under anchored ships. There were so many of them now, with fuel bunkers dry and decks crammed with escapees. From the bottom they appeared to us as clouds would to solbreeders. We found a resting place under the semi-darkness of an oil tanker. Ironically it was anchored over a sunken pleasure boat. We sat resting with our backs against the yacht's broken hull, both of us too shocked and depleted to stir. Only when the shadow's movement forced us to change positions did I notice the extent of Laila's injuries.

Her body had been almost completely roasted. How many times had I warned her against sleeping in the nude! I stared into the mask of horror that had been her face, at the mist of minute, charred particles that lifted lazily from naked white bone. She had always been so vain, so obsessed with her unblemished beauty. That was why she had turned us so many centuries ago. Her worst nightmare had been the loss of her appearance. I could only be grateful that the seawater masked my tears. I forced a brave smile and drew my arm around her near skeletal shoulder. As her body shook in my embrace, one black, carbonized arm raised to point in the direction of Penai beach.

The subdead were coming, walking out of the silt-formed fog. Of course they did not notice us, passing without even the slightest recognition. Penang island, the last human refuge, was their only target now. We watched them silently, too debilitated to even move out of their way. One came close enough to trip over my outstretched leg. As it fell in slow motion, I extended my free arm to catch it. I'm not sure why I did that, neither did Laila. She looked at me quizzically and, with equal confusion, I shrugged. The burnt, cracked remnants of her lips pulled back into a smile, so much so that her lower one split in two. I pretended not to notice. I smiled back and held her close. We sat motionless, watching the cavalcade of cadavers until the ocean's orange surface faded from blue, to orange, to purple, and finally to blessed black.

We came ashore several hours after sunset, into the teeth of a raging battle. Now it was my turn to carry Laila. Limp and trembling, she clung to my neck as we sprinted past the beachhead fray. I found a deep, secure burrow within the rubble of Georgetown's fallen Komptar Tower. Its inaccessibility from both solbreeders and daylight was all we could have asked for now. With Laila resting silently on her back, steam perpetually rising from her wounds, all I could do was hold the mangled remnants of her hand and whisper the faint lullabies of a distant, almost forgotten youth.

We remained secluded in our ramshackle burrow for seven nights, Laila recuperating slowly while I foraged after dark for blood. There were still quite a few living humans left in Penang, fighting bravely as wave after wave of subdead rose from the sea. Those nights witnessed the absolute best of their species, and absolute worst of ours.

There is no greater nightmare than watching one of your own kill another. The victim was smaller and weaker. She was murdered by a larger male over what I could see was a barely conscious meal. Madness? There were still so many other living solbreeders. Why fight over this one? Madness. So many human minds had collapsed. Why should we be any different? I observed several other murders during those seven nights, including one that took place for no apparent reason. There were two evenly matched males, each tearing and biting and trying to extract each other's hearts. At the time I believed I could almost see their insanity, a living entity of pure dementia that bashed my brethren together like the war toys of a sadistic child. I would only wonder later if their duel might not be homicide but rather mutually agreed suicide.

Taking one's own life was nothing new to my people. Immortality has always bred despair. Once every century or so we would hear stories of someone 'walking into a bonfire'. I had never personally seen this action. Now I became its nightly spectator. In tears or silence, I watched so many of my species, so many beautiful, strong, seemingly invincible specimens simply step into burning buildings. I also bore witness to several acts of 'suicide by subdead' as several of my friends willingly sank their fangs into the walking plague's putrid flesh. While their howls of agony tortured my waking hours, nothing so tore at my heart as the night I found Nguyen.

He was strolling, for lack of a better word, down the middle of Macallister Street, amidst the remains of subdead and solbreeder corpses. His face was peaceful, almost chipper. He did not seem to notice me at first. His eyes remained locked on the luminous east. 'Nguyen!' I called nervously, not wanting to waste any more time getting 'home.' Scrounging was becoming difficult and I was eager to return my catch to Laila before the sun rose. 'Nguyen!' I shouted with growing impatience. Finally on my third call, the elder existentialist turned. He looked up at me standing on the rubble of the old mosque and gave me a friendly wave, 'What are you…' I began but was quickly silenced by his answer. 'Just walking into the dawn.' His tone implied an action both obvious and expected. 'Just walking into the dawn.'

I did not mention what I'd seen to Laila, nor did I tell her about any of the horrors beyond our little cave. As she fed off the barely breathing sustenance, I forced the brightest smile possible and repeated the words I'd rehearsed in my head. 'We're going to be fine,' I began, 'I know how to get out of this.' The notion had come to me that first day under the ship, and had germinated rapidly over the past several nights.

'Husbandry,' I began, and her still mending eyebrows crinkled in wonder. 'That's how the solbreeders became the dominant species on the planet. At some point they switched from hunting animals to domesticating them. That's what we're going to do!' Before she could speak, I placed a hand to her regenerating lips. 'Just consider it! There are still hundreds of vessels that must contain thousands of solbreeders. All we need to do is take one of those ships by force. We'll just sail our livestock to an island somewhere. There are millions of them close by. All we have to do is find one large enough to construct a solbreeder ranch! Some of those islands might even have ranches on them already! Well, the humans don't think they're ranches, they think they're havens. But wait till we arrive! One night of violence, just enough to eliminate the alphas in the herd. The rest will follow. They've been through so much they'll be ripe for the taking! We'll begin breeding solbreeders! We'll keep weeding out the troublesome ones, keep fattening and hobbling the submissive ones. We might even breed out much of their intelligence over time. And we have all the time in the world! The subdead won't last forever, you've seen them rotting, eh? Eh? How long can they last, a few years, a few decades? We'll just wait them out, safe on our island coral, with our self-sustaining blood supply or better, even better, we go to Borneo or New

Guinea! There must still be some human tribes out there that haven't been touched by this holocaust! We can become their rulers, their deities! We won't need to tend them, or slaughter them, they'll do it all themselves, and all for the love of their new Gods! We can do it! You'll see! We can and we WILL!'

At that point I legitimately believed everything I espoused. It didn't matter how we were going to find and capture either a ship or an island. It didn't matter how we were going to keep this mystical 'herd' of solbreeders captive, or healthy, or even fed. I'd only just thought of the Borneo-New Guinea option and so those details seemed even more trivial than human husbandry. What mattered was how deeply I wanted to believe in myself, and how deeply I wanted Laila to believe in me.

I should have recognized the smile on her face, how closely it resembled Nguyen's. I should have restrained her that instant, with steel and concrete or even my own body. I should have never gone to sleep that day. I should not have been surprised at what I found the next evening. Laila, my sister, my friend, my strong, beautiful, eternal night sky. How long had it been since we were children of the beating heart, laughing and playing beneath the warmth of the noonday sun? How long had it been since I followed her into the darkness? How long would it be before I followed her into the light?

The nights are quiet now. The screams and fires have long faded. The subdead are everywhere now, shuffling aimless as far as the eye can see. It has been almost three weeks since I hunted the last remaining humans in the city, almost four months since my beloved Laila turned to ash. At least part of my ranching strategy has taken form. Some solbreeders still exist on nearby anchored ships, living off fish and rainwater, and some hope of eventual rescue. Although I feed as sparingly as possible, their numbers continue to diminish. I have calculated another few months at the most before I drain the last of them white. Even if I had half the knowledge, or will, to implement my plan of domestication, there still would not be enough left for a sustainable herd. Facts can be a most cruel master, and as Nguyen once said, 'I've done the math.'

Maybe some of my kind have taken on similar 'husbandry' projects. Maybe some have managed to succeed. The world has suddenly become a very, very big place, and across its vast horizon, there are always possibilities. I suppose I could try to strike out in search of these survivalist colonies, with a hobbled solbreeder or two under my arms. Perhaps I could find some means of keeping them alive for a bit, giving them food and water, and chaining them together during the day while I burrowed. I remember one of the Sirenes discussing a similar idea for his sojourn. If rationed carefully and traveling at maximum speed, I might even cover a good amount of nearby land. And what I might discover is what keeps me rooted to the island of Penang. At least in ignorance there can be fantasy, and these nights, fantasy is all I have left.

In my fantasy, repugnant mobile carcasses will not inherit the earth. In my fantasy, children of both night and day will somehow survive long enough for the subdead to dissolve into dust. That is why I have preserved these memories, on paper and wood and even glass, as I have emulated from a human 'apocalypse novel'. In my fantasy I am not simply wasting my final nights with fruitless, Malthusian ramblings. My words will serve as a guide, a warning, and the eventual salvation of the race known to all as Vampires. I am not the final flickering of a light that had allowed itself to be extinguished. I am not the last dancer in the extinction parade.

Great Wall:
A Story from the Zombie War

The following interview was conducted by the author as part of his official duties with the United Nations Commission for Postwar Data Collection. Although excerpts have appeared in the official UN report, the interview in its entirety was omitted from Brook's personal publication, now entitled World War Z, *due to bureaucratic misman- agement by UN archivists. The following is a first-hand account of a survivor of the great crisis many now refer to simply as 'The Zombie War'.*

THE GREAT WALL: SECTION 3947-B, SHAANXI, CHINA

Liu Huafeng began her career as a sales girl at the Takashimaya department store in Taiyun and now owns a small general store near the sight of its former location. This weekend, as on the first weekend of every month, is her reserve duty. Armed with a radio, a flare gun, binoculars and a 'DaDao', a modernized version of the ancient Chinese broadsword, she patrols her five kilometre stretch of the Great Wall with nothing but the 'the wind and my memories' for company.

This section of the Wall, the section I worked on, stretches from Yulin to Shemnu. It had originally been built by the Xia Dynasty, constructed of compacted sand and reed-lined earth encased on both sides by a thick outer shell of fired mud brick. It never appeared on any tourist postcards. It could never have hoped to rival sections of the iconic Ming-Era stone 'dragon spine'. It was dull and was functional, and by the time we began the reconstruction, it had almost completely vanished.

Thousands of years of erosion, storms and desertification, had taken a drastic toll. The effects of human 'progress' had been equally destructive. Over the centuries, locals had used – looted – its bricks for building materials. Modern road construction had done its part too, removing entire sections that interfered with 'vital' overland traffic. And, of course, what nature and peacetime development had begun, the crisis, the infestation and the subsequent civil war finished within the course of several months. In some places, all that was left were crumbling hummocks of compact filler. In many places, there was nothing at all.

I didn't know about the new government's plan to restore the Great Wall for our national defence. At first, I didn't even know I was part of the effort. In those early days there were so many different languages – local dialects that could have been birdsong for all the sense it made to me. The night I arrived, all you could see were torches and headlights of a few broken down cars. I had been walking for nine days by this point. I was tired, frightened. I didn't know what I had found at first, only that the scurrying shapes in front of me were human. I don't know how long I stood there, but someone on a work gang spotted me. He ran over and started to chatter excitedly. I tried to show him that I didn't understand. He became frustrated, pointing at what looked like a construction sight behind him, a mass of activity that stretched left and right out into the darkness. Again, I shook my head, gesturing to my ears and shrugging like a fool. He sighed angrily, then raised his hand towards me. I saw he was holding a brick. I thought he was going to hit me with it so I started to back away. He then shoved the brick in my hands, motioned to the construction sight, and shoved me towards it.

I got within arm's length of the nearest worker before he snatched the brick away. This man was from Taiyuan. I understood him clearly. 'Well, what the fuck are you waiting for?' He snarled at me, 'We need more! Go! GO!' And that is how I was 'recruited' to work on the new Great Wall of China.

She gestures to the uniform concrete edifice.

It didn't look at all like this that first frantic spring. What you are seeing are the subsequent renovations and reinforcements that adhere to late and postwar standards. We didn't have anything close to these materials back then. Most of our surviving infrastructure was trapped on the wrong side of the wall.

'On the south side?'

Yes, on the side that used to be safe, on the side that the Wall, that every Wall, from the Xia to the Ming, was originally built to protect. The walls used to be a border between the haves and have-nots, between southern prosperity and northern barbarism. Even in modern times, certainly in this part of the country, most of our arable land, as well as our factories, our roads, rail lines and airstrips, almost everything we needed to undertake such a monumental task, was on the wrong side.

'I've heard that some industrial machinery was transported north during the evacuation.'

Only what could be carried on foot, and only what was in immediate proximity to the construction sight. Nothing farther than, say, twenty kilometres, nothing beyond the immediate battle lines or the isolated zones deep in infested territory.

The most valuable resource we could take from the nearby towns was the materials used to construct the towns themselves: wood, metal, cinderblocks, bricks – some of the very same bricks that had originally been pilfered from the wall. All of it went into the mad patchwork, mixed in with what could be manufactured quickly on sight. We used timber from the Great Green Wall* reforestation project, pieces of furniture and abandoned vehicles. Even the desert sand beneath our

---

* The Great Green Wall: a pre-war environmental restoration project intended to halt desertification.

feet was mixed with rubble to form part of the core or else refined and heated for blocks of glass.

'Glass?'

Large, like so. *She draws an imaginary shape in the air, roughly twenty centimetres in length, width and depth.* An engineer from Shijiazhuang had the idea. Before the war, he had owned a glass factory and he realized that since this province's most abundant resources are coal and sand, why not use them both? A massive industry sprung up almost overnight, to manufacture thousands of these large, cloudy bricks. They were thick and heavy, impervious to a zombie's soft, naked fist. 'Stronger than flesh' we used say, and, unfortunately for us, much sharper – sometimes the glazier's assistants would forget to sand down the edges before laying them out for transport.

She pries her hand from the hilt of her sword. The fingers remain curled like a claw. A deep, white scar runs down the width of one palm.

I didn't know to wrap my hands. It cut right through to the bone, severed the nerves. I don't know how I didn't die of infection; so many others did.

It was a brutal, frenzied existence. We knew that every day brought the southern hordes closer, and that any second we delayed might doom the entire effort. We slept, if we did sleep, where we worked. We ate where we worked, pissed and shat right where we worked. Children – the 'Night Soil Cubs' – would hurry by with a bucket, wait while we did our business or else collect our previously discarded filth. We worked like animals, lived like animals. In my dreams I see a thousand faces, the people I worked with but never knew. There wasn't time for social interaction. We spoke mainly in hand gestures and grunts. In my dreams I try to find the time to speak to those alongside me, ask their names, their stories. I have heard that dreams are only in black and white. Perhaps that is true, perhaps I only remember the colours later, the light fringes of a girl whose hair had once been died green, or the soiled pink woman's bathrobe wrapped around a frail old man in tattered silken pajamas. I see their faces almost every night, only the faces of the fallen.

So many died. Someone working at your side would sit down for a moment, just a second to catch their breath, and never rise again. We had what could be described as a medical detail, orderlies with stretchers. There was nothing they could really do except try to get them to the aid station. Most of the time they didn't make it. I carry their suffering and my shame with me each and every day.

'Your shame?'

As they sat, or lay at your feet, you knew you couldn't stop what you were doing, not even for a little compassion, a few kind words, at least make them comfortable enough to wait for the medics. You knew the one thing they wanted, what we all wanted, was water. Water was precious in this part of the province, and almost all we had was used for mixing ingredients into mortar. We were given less than half a cup a day. I carried mine around my neck in a recycled plastic soda bottle. We were under strict orders not to share our ration with the sick and injured. We needed it to keep ourselves working. I understand the logic, but to see someone's broken body curled up amongst the tools and rubble, knowing that the only mercy under heaven was just a little sip of water...

I feel guilty every time I think about it, every time
I quench my thirst, especially because when it came my
time to die, I happened, by sheer chance, to be near the
aid station. I was on glass detail, part of the long, human
conveyor to and from the kilns. I had been on the
project for just under two months; I was starving, fever-
ish, I weighed less than the bricks hanging from either
side of my pole. As I turned to pass the bricks, I stumbled, landing on my face. I felt my two front teeth crack
and tasted the blood. I closed my eyes and thought, 'this
is my time'. I was ready. I wanted it to end. If the
orderlies hadn't been passing by, my wish would have
been granted.

For three days, I lived in shame; resting, washing,
drinking as much water as I wanted while others were
suffering every second on the wall. The doctors told me
that I should stay a few extra days, the bare minimum
to allow my body to recuperate. I would have listened if
I didn't hear the shouts from an orderly at the mouth of
the cave.

'Red Flare!' he was calling. 'RED FLARE!'

Green flares meant an active assault, red meant

overwhelming numbers. Reds had been uncommon, up until that point. I had only seen one, and that was far in the distance near the northern edge of Shemnu. Now they were coming at least once a week. I raced out of the cave, ran all the way back to my section, just in time to see rotting hands and heads begin to poke their way above the unfinished ramparts.

We halt. She looks down at the stones beneath out feet.

Here, right here. They were forming a ramp, using their trodden comrades for elevation. The workers were fending them off with whatever they could, tools and bricks, even bare fists and feet. I grabbed a rammer, an implement used for compacting earth. The rammer is an immense, unruly device, a metre-long metal shaft with horizontal handlebars on one end and a large, cylindrical, supremely heavy stone on the other. The rammer was reserved only for the largest and strongest men in our work gang. I don't know how I managed to lift, aim, and bring it crashing down, over and over, on the heads and faces of the zombies below me…

The military was supposed to be protecting us from

overrun attacks like these, but there just weren't enough soldiers left by that time.

She takes me to the edge of the battlements and points to something roughly a kilometre south of us.

There.

In the distance, I can just make out a stone obelisk rising from an earthen mound.

Underneath that mound is one of our garrison's last main battle tanks. The crew had run out of fuel and was using it as a pillbox. When they ran out of ammunition, they sealed the hatches and prepared to trap themselves as bait. They held on long after their food ran out and their canteens ran dry. 'Fight on!' they would cry over their hand-cranked radio. 'Finish the wall! Protect our people! Finish the wall!' The last of them, the seventeen-year-old driver, held out for thirty-one days. You couldn't even see the tank by then, buried under a small mountain of zombies that suddenly moved away as they sensed that boy's last breath.

By that time, we had almost finished our section of the Great Wall, but the isolated attacks were ending, and the massive, ceaseless, million-strong assault swarms began. If we had had to contend with those numbers in the beginning, if the heroes of the southern cities hadn't shed their blood to buy us time...

The new government knew it had to distance itself from the one it had just overthrown. It had to establish some kind of legitimacy with our people, and the only way to do that was to speak the truth. The isolated zones weren't 'tricked' into becoming decoys like in so many other countries. They were asked, openly and honestly, to remain behind while others fled. It would be a personal choice, one that every citizen would have to make for themselves. My mother, she made it for me.

We had been hiding on the second floor of what used to be our five bedroom house in what used to be one of Taiyuan's most exclusive suburban enclaves. My little brother was dying, bitten when my father had sent him out to look for food. He was lying in my parent's bed, shaking, unconscious. My father was sitting by his side, rocking slowly back and forth. Every few minutes he would call out to us. 'He's getting better! See, feel his forehead. He's getting better!' The refugee train was passing right by our house. Civil Defence Deputies were checking each door to find out who was going and who was staying. My mother already had a small bag of my things packed; clothes, food, a good pair of walking shoes, my father's pistol with the last three bullets. She was combing my hair in the mirror, the way she used to do when I was a little girl. She told me to stop crying and that some day soon they would rejoin me up north. She had that smile, that frozen, lifeless smile she only showed for father and his friends. She had it for me now, as I lowered myself down our broken staircase.

Liu pauses, takes a breath, and lets her claw rest on the hard stone.

Three months, that is how long it took us to complete the entire Great Wall. From Jingtai in the western mountains to the Great Dragon head on the Shanhaiguan Sea. It was never breached, never overrun. It gave us the breathing space we needed to finally consolidate our population and construct a wartime economy. We were the last country to adopt the Redeker plan, so long after the rest of the world, and just in time for the Honolulu Conference. So much time, so many lives, all wasted. If the Three Gorges Dam hadn't collapsed, if that other wall hadn't fallen, would we have resurrected this one? Who knows. Both are monuments to our shortsightedness, our arrogance, our disgrace.

They say that so many workers died building the original walls that a human life was lost for every mile. I don't know if it was true of that time…

Her claw pats the stone.

But it is now.

NOW AVAILABLE

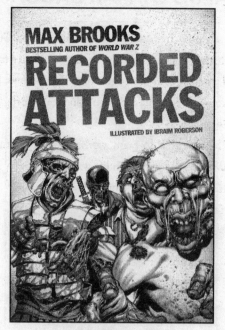

Recorded Attacks
MAX BROOKS

With illustrations by Ibraim Roberson

£10.99 ISBN 980715643051

THOSE WHO DON'T LEARN FROM HISTORY ARE CONDEMNED TO REPEAT IT.
From the Stone Age to the information age, the undead have threatened to engulf the human race. They're coming. And they're hungry.

DON'T WAIT FOR THEM TO COME TO YOU!
This is the graphic novel the fans demanded: major zombie attacks from the dawn of humanity. On the African savannas, against the legions of ancient Rome, on the high seas with Francis Drake... every civilization has faced them. Here are the grisly and heroic stories — complete with eye-popping artwork that pulsates with the hideous faces of the undead.

ORGANISE BEFORE THEY RISE!
By immersing ourselves in past horror we may yet prevail over the coming outbreak...

ALSO BY MAX BROOKS

World War Z
An Oral History of the Zombie War

£9.99 ISBN 980715637036

NOW A MAJOR HOLLYWOOD FILM

The Zombie War came unthinkably close to eradicating humanity. Driven by the urgency of preserving the acid-etched firsthand experiences of the survivors from those apocalyptic years, Max Brooks travelled the world recording the testimony of men, women, and children who came face-to-face with the living, or at least the undead, hell of that time. *World War Z* is the terrifying result.

'An absolute must have... Brooks infuses his writing with such precise detail and authenticity, one wonders if he knows something we don't' Simon Pegg

'When the zombie apocalypse arrives, we'll be at Max Brooks's house... as a horror story, it's exciting. As a parable, it's terrifying' *Empire* *****

ALSO BY MAX BROOKS

The Zombie Survival Guide
Complete Protection from the Living Dead

£8.99 ISBN 980715633182

OVER 1 MILLION COPIES SOLD

This book is your key to survival against the hordes of the undead stalking you right now. Fully illustrated, it covers everything you need to know, from how to understand zombie behaviour to survival in any territory or terrain. It might just save your life.

'A bloody-minded, straight-laced manual for evading the grasp of the undead' *Time Out*

'A tome you start reading for fun and then at page 50 you go out and buy a machete just to be on the safe side' *New York Post*